Published by Paper Seed Press, LLC, 2024
Iona, ID, USA

Publisher's Cataloging-in-Publication Data
Names: Atkison, Jeana, 1991- , author. | Oza, Devika, 1994- , illustrator.

Title: How to eat a cupcake / Jeana Atkison ; Devika Oza
Description: Iona, ID : Paper Seed Press, 2024. | Includes 36 color illustrations. | Audience: Ages 3 to 8. | Summary: Charlie likes to be extra careful, but sometimes it makes him feel...different. When he is invited to a very unique birthday party, Charlie learns the importance and joy of differences.
Identifiers: LCCN 2023951452 | ISBN 9781963149005 (hardback) | ISBN 9781963149029 (paperback) | ISBN 9781963149012 (ebook)
Subjects: LCSH: Cupcakes – Juvenile fiction. | Birthday parties – Juvenile fiction. | Children with disabilities – Juvenile fiction. | Social acceptance – Juvenile fiction. | Families – Juvenile fiction. | Friendship – Juvenile fiction. | BISAC: JUVENILE FICTION / Disabilities. | JUVENILE FICTION / Social Themes / Friendship. | JUVENILE FICTION / Family / General.
Classification: LCC PZ7.1 A85 2024 | DDC [E]--dc23
LC record available at https://lccn.loc.gov/2023951452

How to Eat a Cupcake

Written by
JEANA ATKISON

Illustrated by
DEVIKA OZA

Published by Paper Seed Press, LLC

An dr ew
Sa rah

To my loving husband who always buys me cupcakes, and to my children who eat them.
– J.A.

To my chocolate loving Dadaji.
– D.O.

My name is Charlie.

But, most people call me
"Careful Charlie" for. . . well. . .

. . .obvious reasons.

Sometimes it makes me feel. . . *different.*

To Tom
To Luke
To Rosie & Ruby
To Ben

TAP TAP
4

I read every line of Sarah's invitation.

Twice.

Sarah's party was going to be at a bakery which seemed. . . *different*. I thought carefully about whether or not to go.

Café
OPEN
PASTA
ro

Dingle
Ring
PASTRIES
croissant
Chocolate
slice
Pineapple
slice
Double chocolate
frosting slice

The bakery smelled delicious! I read every line on the menu.

Twice.

I made it just in time for the cupcakes. "For my favorite sister," Andrew said, handing Sarah a special birthday cupcake.

He sounded a little different, but no one seemed to mind. Maybe the rest of the party would be more normal. . .
but then I saw Ben.

Ben had split his cupcake in half and put the bottom on the top!

"This way I don't get frosting on my fingers while I use one hand to move my wheelchair." Ben said.

Then I saw Rosie.

She was eating just the frosting! There were so many different things happening at this party! But, everyone was happy.

Then I saw Ruby.

"What are you doing?" I asked.

"I'm swapping the frosting from two cupcakes to make two new cupcakes. Mwahahaha!" Ruby cackled.

I laughed with Ruby, being a cupcake scientist looked like fun!

Andrew laughed, too. His laugh made me smile.

"Ruby, that is super messy. You need to eat your cupcake like me," said Tom.

Ruby's smile fell.

"I think Ruby's way of eating a cupcake is great!" Sarah said as she picked each sprinkle off her frosting. Andrew shoved an entire cupcake into his mouth and grinned.

Ruby's way? I thought. I realized each of my friends had eaten a cupcake differently, in their *own way*. And they were happy.

Except for Luke.

Luke's plate was empty.

"I wish I could eat a cupcake," said Luke. "I'm allergic to gluten."

"I'm glad you are careful," Sarah told me.
"Only you could help Luke."

It turns out, being "Careful Charlie" isn't bad.
What makes me different makes me special.

But sometimes, even I like to be a little. . .

messY!

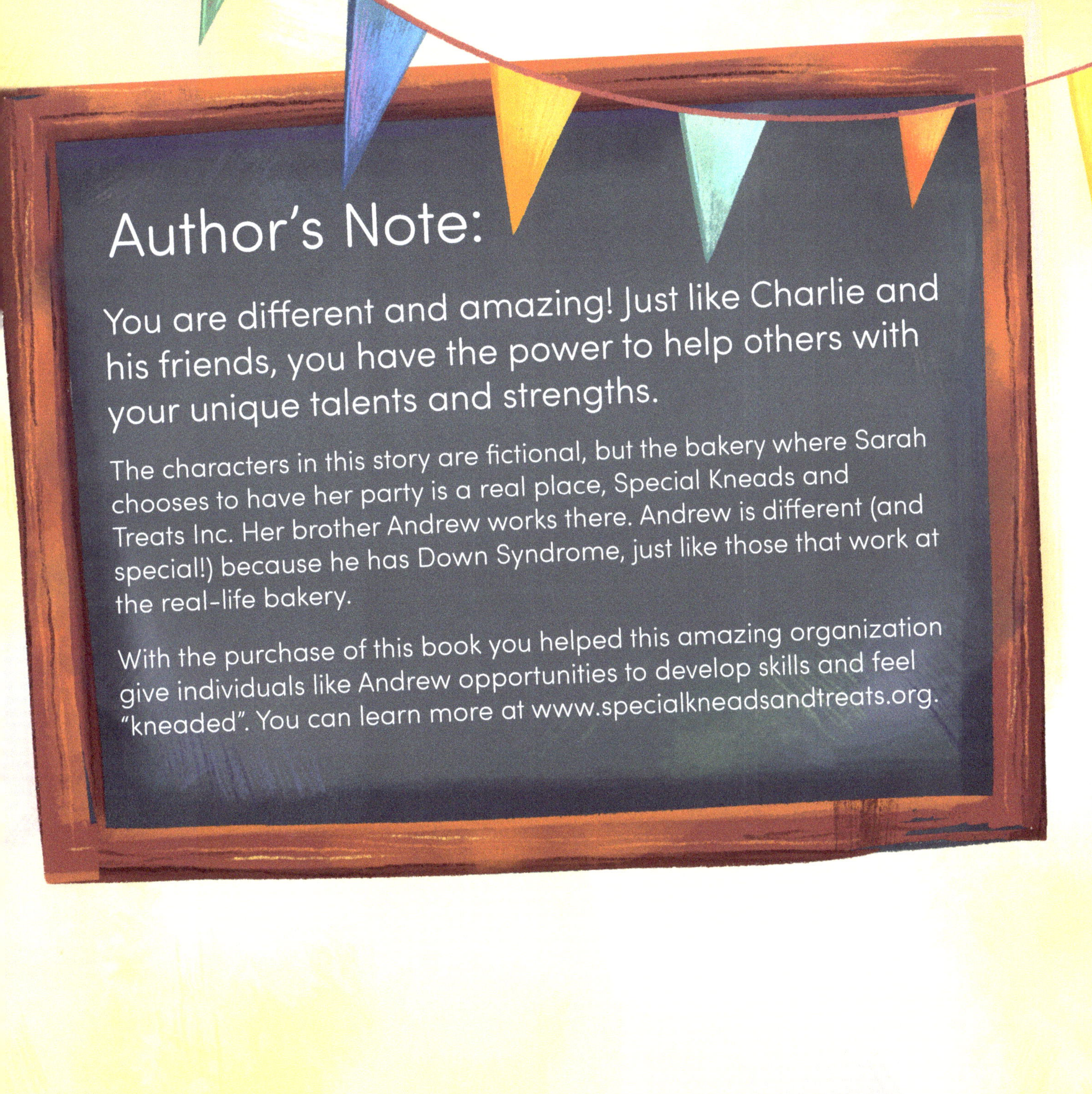

Author's Note:

You are different and amazing! Just like Charlie and his friends, you have the power to help others with your unique talents and strengths.

The characters in this story are fictional, but the bakery where Sarah chooses to have her party is a real place, Special Kneads and Treats Inc. Her brother Andrew works there. Andrew is different (and special!) because he has Down Syndrome, just like those that work at the real-life bakery.

With the purchase of this book you helped this amazing organization give individuals like Andrew opportunities to develop skills and feel "kneaded". You can learn more at www.specialkneadsandtreats.org.

DISCOVER WHAT MAKES YOU
DIFFERENT!

My name

Favorite Activity

Hobbies

I love myself because I

This is me

I am good at

ADDITIONAL RESOURCES:

Visit www.paperseedpress.com to download the FREE *How to Eat a Cupcake* Activity Pack and continue the fun and learning with discovery pages, lesson plans, riddles, STEM activities and more!

DISCUSSION QUESTIONS:

1. Which character in the story do you feel is most similar to you? Why?

2. Which character in the story do you feel is most different to you? Why?

3. In the story, Ben uses a wheelchair. Have you ever seen someone that needed a wheelchair? How do you think their life might be different than yours?

4. Now that you know your differences can be your greatest strengths, what are some things that make you different and how could you help others with those unique talents and strengths?

5. Why do you think we sometimes see differences as bad? What can we do to be more accepting of differences in ourselves and others?

Thank You!

We sincerely hope you enjoyed reading *How to Eat a Cupcake*. Please consider leaving an honest review of this book on Amazon or Goodreads. Help spread the word and support our mission of giving back by raising kind kids and helping non-profits with their unique missions of kindness.